D1603797

Life...
Real
&
Imagined

Life...
Real &
Imagined

A Collection of Short Stories by
Anthony S. Markellis

SHIRES ✿ PRESS

4869 Main Street • P.O. Box 2200
Manchester Center, VT 05255
www.northshire.com

Life... Real & Imagined

ISBN: 978-1-60571- 503-1

Building Community, One Book at a Time

*A family-owned, independent bookstore in
Manchester Center, VT since 1976 and
Saratoga Springs, NY since 2013.
We are committed to excellence in bookselling. The
Northshire Bookstore's mission is to serve as a resource
for information, ideas, and entertainment while
honoring the needs of customers, staff, and community.*

Printed in the United States of America

Table of Contents

Preface

WE ARE ALL ALIKE IN SO MANY WAYS, but that's not what makes life interesting, is it? It's the differences between us that make life worth living. These stories deal with people of many ages, races, nationalities, religions and walks of life, and are one man's attempt to understand them. Some of these tales are eyewitness accounts of actual events (if perhaps embellished a bit); and some of them are pure fiction. I'll leave it to you to decide which ones are which.

I hope you will enjoy these stories as much as I have enjoyed putting them together.

Dedicated to the memory of
Constantine and Victoria Markellis,
who made sure I grew up curious
about everything and everybody.

Whenever possible,
keep your
eyes and ears open
and your mouth shut.

Introduction

WHAT AN EAR THIS MAN HAS! LISTENING to Tony Markellis play his music, you can't go wrong. Over several decades, I've heard his bass making some of the greats even better. And after he leaves the stage, his ears don't turn off. He captures the spoken word as it belongs to each individual. Some dialects and psyches might sound familiar to you. Others hail from tiny cultural ecosystems you might never visit.

Early in my life, I got to know Tony in upstate New York. Over coffee, steak and eggs, or some wildly (to me at that time) exotic and expensive meals, he told me about people I couldn't wait to meet. He also introduced me to music I would never have otherwise heard (not to mention a worm-dispensing machine called the Vend-a-Bait).

Pull up a chair. These are tales that sometimes show what divides us, but also what unites us. They're stories of character, of mistakes, triumphs, and vulnerability. Pretend he told them to you over a good meal at a place like Hattie's Chicken Shack or the old Sam's.

And if you're not fortunate enough to have Tony in front of you telling a yarn like he does, watch out. He might be right behind you. Listening.

Ellen Jordis Lewis

The Hot Breakfast
(Trilogy, Part 1)

THE TRUCKER SMILED AS HE INHALED the aroma of a table heaped with biscuits and gravy, scrambled eggs, a T-bone steak, cheese grits, hash browns and black coffee. There weren't many things he loved more than a hot breakfast, and spread out before him this morning was the first one he had seen since leaving his Montana home nearly two weeks earlier. He had lost track of the number of times he and his Peterbilt had crisscrossed the Continental Divide.

As he often did, this morning the trucker had spent the few hours before dawn sleeping in the cab of his truck, waiting for the lumberyard to open so he could deliver the flatbed of plywood before driving across town to pick up one last load that he would drop in Idaho on his way home. Today he was celebrating a particularly well-planned and profitable trip—he figured that after four or five more like this one he would finally have his truck paid off in full.

He surveyed the spread, deciding where to start. As he lifted the first forkful of the golden-hued grits toward his mouth, his hand froze as he heard the quiet yet forcefully whispered hiss of a female voice from the high-backed booth behind him. *"Damn it! That's the second glass of juice you've spilled this morning. If you think I'm gonna put up with any more of your childish bullshit, mister, you've got another thing coming. You're lucky I don't just leave you on the side of the road for the buzzards to pick clean!"*

The trucker was a kind and decent man. He had always made a point of not meddling in other people's affairs, but being himself a father of three, he couldn't stand to hear anyone talk to their children that way. He cleared his throat, put down his fork, stood up to his full six feet, four inches and said calmly but firmly as he faced the angry woman in the next booth, "Pardon me, ma'am, but there's no cause to talk to him that way. Kids will be kids."

It was only after he had spoken his piece that he noticed out of the corner of his eye that the second party in the other booth was no child, but rather a tiny, weather-beaten old man in a worn brown suit coat. His face was framed by silver-white braids descending from the flat brim of a straw cowboy hat adorned by a single eagle feather.

"Just how's this any of your business, cowboy?" asked the stout middle-aged Native American woman.

"Well, ma'am, I guess it's not, but do you have to be so hard on the old fella?" he asked.

After glaring at the well-intentioned trucker for what seemed to him an eternity, she said, "Fine. If you think you know so damn much, he's all yours." She slapped their breakfast check into his hand and pushed past him, muttering loudly to no one in particular, *"Kids will be kids*. Ha!" as she stormed out the door.

The confused trucker looked at the door, and back at the sunbaked little man, at the check in his hand, back at his own untouched breakfast, and back at the man. The sound of spinning tires throwing gravel ripped through the air as the pickup truck fishtailed out of the parking lot and onto the blacktop.

"She's coming back, isn't she?" the trucker asked the old man.

"Prob'ly not," was his quiet reply. "She's pretty damn mad."

But then, this wasn't the trucker's problem. All he wanted this morning was to eat that magnificent breakfast while it was still hot. "Well, okay then, old timer—good luck," he said as he sat back down.

As he once again picked up his fork, a reedy sigh from the next booth blew through him like the first wind of winter. The trucker slowly put the fork back down on his plate as he thought about what, if anything, he should do next. Besides maybe picking up the old man's breakfast check, did he owe him anything? He stood back up and asked, "Say, mister, just how far from here do you live?"

"About five miles up the road—on the mixed-nation rez," he replied without looking up.

"Is there someone you can call?" asked the trucker.

"Nope. Just that good-for-nothing daughter," he said.

Still hoping to get a bite of his breakfast while it was warm, the trucker invited the old man to come and join him in his booth for a cup of coffee.

"Maybe—I gotta think a little first," said the old man.

The trucker sat down and picked up his fork.

As he once again lifted the same bite of grits toward his mouth, he sensed someone standing at his elbow. "I guess maybe I'll join you," said the diminutive man. "You seem like a nice enough fella."

The trucker now felt bad about eating when the old man had no food in front of him, so he put his fork back down. "If you don't mind telling me, just what got her so riled up this morning?" he asked.

"Your guess is as good as mine," sighed the little man. "She's been getting more and more impatient with me. She's a bad daughter."

"You live with her?"

"Yup, since my wife died five years ago."

"Sorry for your loss," replied the trucker. "Is it just the two of you now?"

"Yup—since she got her husband locked up."

"Locked up? For what?" asked the trucker.

"Oh, nothin' *he* done," replied the old man. "She's a bad wife. As usual, she started some shit, and he was just too dumb to get out of the way of it. The neighbors called the police and she made it look like it was all his fault. I liked him, too. He was always nice to me—he bought me chew and candy. He's a white man, but he's more of a Injun than most of the rest of 'em out there—he's got a big heart. They coulda lived in a nice house in town, but he actually chose to come out and live with us on the reservation. Looks like he's gonna be locked up for a coupla years."

"Look," said the trucker, "I have to pick up a load across town in the next hour, and if I'm not mistaken, I drive past that reservation on my way out of town. Can I give you a ride home?"

"No, thanks," answered the Indian. "I ain't goin' back out there."

"But you have to go home sometime."

After a few moments of silence, the old man asked, "Was you ever in the service?"

"Yeah, the Marines—in Vietnam," replied the trucker. "Why do you ask?"

"You know," said the old man, "I lived all my life on that damn rez—except when I was in the army."

After quickly estimating the old man's age, the trucker asked, "World War II?"

"Yup, in the South Pacific—when I was eighteen. That was the first time."

"The first time?"

"Yup. I never seen the ocean before. What a sight!"

He added, "I went to Korea six years after that."

"Damn—that's a lot of war," replied the trucker, shaking his head.

"Yup. Then I went to Vietnam too—twelve years later."

"Jesus, old timer …"

"You know, I fought in three wars against people that looked more like me than the rest of the guys in my own army did. I didn't have nothin' against none of them foreign boys, neither, but there I was. And what do you suppose I got for my trouble? I got passed over for promotions and decorations. The men in my platoon, some of whose worthless hides I saved more than once, called me "Chief." They never once called me by my name, just "Chief." And then I got to come back here and live on this dried up piece of dirt and watch my wife and all my old friends die off, and end up with nothin' but a mean daughter to show for it all. If you ask me, she done me a favor by dumping me here."

"Why the hell's she so mean, anyway?" asked the trucker.

"Oh, who knows?" replied the old man. "But I'll tell you this much—if a rattler was ever to bite her, someone better get poor Brother Snake to the vet right away, 'cuz otherwise, he ain't long for this world."

They had a good laugh—it was the first light moment they had shared.

"So, what are you gonna do?" asked the younger man. "If you sit here for a while, will one of your friends eventually stop by and get you?"

"Nope. Like I told you—they're all dead," he explained.

"But, you can't just stay here," said the trucker,

who was now becoming truly concerned for the old man's welfare.

After a bit of a pause, the old man said, "I'm a medicine chief—you know what that is?"

"No, I guess not," said the trucker.

"A little bit priest and a little bit doctor," he explained. "In the old days, I was important—people listened to what I had to say. Now I'm the last old one left, and the kids don't give a damn about the old ways anymore. I just sit around on the front porch all day, watchin' the prairie dogs dodge the tumbleweeds. I might as well be dead."

"Now, that's no way to talk," the trucker replied.

"Well, that's the way it is," said the Indian.

"What're you gonna do?" asked the trucker.

After a few moments, the old man suggested, "I could go with you."

"What do you mean, 'go with me'?" asked the surprised trucker.

"Where you headed to?" asked the Indian.

"I've got to pick up a flatbed full of re-bar and drive it up to a construction site in Boise, then I'm headed home to Montana," said the trucker. "I get to spend a whole week at home with my wife before I have to go out again."

"That sounds nice," said the old man. "I've always wanted to see that Big Sky Country before I die. Your wife—is she a good cook?"

"As a matter of fact, yes she is, but..."

"Well then, what're we sittin' 'round here for?" he asked.

"Look here, pard," said the trucker, "you seem like a nice enough fella, and I'm real sorry for your troubles, but I can't just take you home with me."

"Why not?" asked the Indian.

"Because I just met you!" replied the exasperated trucker.

"I just met you, too, and I'm willing to risk it!" said the old man.

"My wife would have my scalp..." started the trucker, without thinking.

The old man laughed. "You married to a Injun?"

"No—sorry—that didn't come out quite right," he stammered, more than a little embarrassed.

"Don't worry about it, cowboy—it was pretty funny," he said with a grin. He added playfully, "If she don't like Injuns, she don't like Injuns."

"Oh, come on—it's nothin' like that. It's just that the kids are all finally grown and out of the house, so when I'm gone she's there all by herself. She counts the hours 'til I come home. If I was to just show up with a stranger—any kind of stranger—man, oh man…"

"Scalped?"

"Yep."

The two sat in silence for a minute.

"You gonna eat them eggs?" asked the old man.

"Nope," replied the trucker, having given up on his breakfast altogether. "Help yourself."

"They're cold," observed the old man after his first bite.

"Do tell," said the trucker.

"How come you ordered so much food if you

wasn't gonna eat it?" asked the old man, shaking his head in disgust. "What a waste."

"Yeah, that's for sure," agreed the trucker.

"So," said the old man. "I guess we better get going—we got a long drive."

The trucker stood and sighed deeply, "Yep, I reckon so."

<u>The Family Business</u>

"**H**OW ABOUT THIS ONE HERE?" ASKED the younger of the two black men as they strolled casually down the middle of the deserted street.

"No, boy—not this one. Not none of these on this block."

"Why not? It's a quiet, dead-end street. Ain't no cops gonna cruise by."

"Son, look at these places—just take a good look," said the older man.

"What am I supposed to be lookin' at?" asked the boy, furrowing his brow as he scanned one side of the street and then the other.

"Look at what's in the yards and on the porches," responded the man, his tone becoming gruff.

"Cars and lawnmowers and barbecue grills—so?" asked the boy.

"Boy, if you're gonna be in the thievin' business, you better be payin' more attention," replied the older man, emphatically.

"To what?"

"To *everything*, boy!" His patience was wearing thin. "What do you see?"

"Like I said, man—cars and lawnmowers."

"Not just cars and lawnmowers, you knuckle-head! Pickup trucks—*rusty* pickup trucks. And old lawn-mowers with parts missin'. And greasy barbecue grills and dog chains 'round the tree. This ain't up the hill where the doctors and lawyers got the Mercedes and them yappy little Mexican dogs. No, boy, these peo-ple here is rednecks. Squirrel-eatin', chaw-chewin', NASCAR-watchin' *RED NECKS!* With *GUNS!* Guns and big, mean, raggedy dogs! These crackers here ain't got shit, but they willin' to shoot your ass to keep you from stealin' it! You understand? You'll be lyin' in the driveway shot full of holes, just prayin' to the Lord that someone call the police before they let them nasty dogs out to chew up what's left of you!"

"Uh-huh, I see what you mean," replied the boy flatly. After a moment of silence he added, "Maybe we could just grab one of them ridin' mowers when no one's lookin'."

"Bust our ass stealin' a half a ton of rusty junk while Jethro uses us for target practice? And do what with it—ride it downtown and pawn it? I swear, you get stupider *every god damn day!*"

The otherwise oblivious boy's feelings were hurt. "Why you always gotta disagree with everything I say?"

"I'll tell you why," replied the old man. "Because everything you say is always *wrong*, that's why!"

Fatigued by this seemingly eternal exchange, the old man added, "Boy, you wanna be dog food, be my guest—but do it on your own time."

<u>Tears Are Tears</u>

MANOLITO HERNANDEZ SHIVERS AS HE stands waiting for the bus in the icy wind.

"How did I find myself in this cold place?" he asks himself.

He came north in the summer, when the climate was not unlike that in which he had grown up. Now the snow piles up and the slush soaks his shoes, which, like him, are better suited for warmer weather.

Manolito washes vegetables and peels potatoes in a restaurant. He shares a one-bedroom apartment with four other boys from Oaxaca, one of whom is a dishwasher in the same kitchen, and another a busboy. The other two work similar jobs at a restaurant a couple of blocks from the one where Manolito is employed.

What he doesn't spend on rice, beans and his share of the rent, he sends home to his mother every Friday. Although the money pays her bills, it cannot dry the tears she cries for her son so far away in such a cold place. While it could be argued that tears are tears, hers soak her apron; Manolito's just freeze on his cheeks. He never cried in Oaxaca; there was never anything to cry about. There was no work there, but Manolito had his family, he had the warmth of the sun, and he had the delicious *tamales* made by his mother and his grandmother.

All five of the boys work with food in one way or another, but not one of them could be mistaken for a chef. They boil beans and rice and toast store-bought *tortillas* on the burner of the gas stove in their stark, mattress-strewn apartment. Occasionally they ride their bicycles or catch the bus to the cluster of strip malls outside of town where there is a choice of three different gringo taco chain restaurants—all of them sad substitutes for the food they grew up eating—but at least there, among somewhat familiar smells, they can meet with more of their countrymen and commiserate about life in the States and how much they miss their homes and their mothers' cooking.

For the time being, the girls don't leave their Oaxacan homes and come to the frozen north—only the boys, some of whom work construction, or do yard work, or work on horse farms. But here, in this town, most of them work behind the scenes in kitchens. At the diner, in the fine dining establishments and even at the local Thai restaurant, when the kitchen door swings open, the face you see toiling over the dish sink is more than likely to be that of a young Oaxacan boy.

Manolito has received news that his father is terribly ill and not likely to survive. He would like more than anything to go visit him before it is too late, but his work visa has expired, and if he were to leave the U.S. he would be unable to return. There is no short-term solution to his problem, but his American girlfriend is pregnant and there is the eventual possibility of marriage and citizenship.

For now, though, his tears still freeze.

A Phone Call

"HELLO—DINER. THIS IS GINNY."

"Oh—hi, Hon."

"Huh?"

"What?"

"It's in your tool box."

"'Cause that's where you told me to put it."

"Well, unless you lost it since yesterday, it's still there."

"Before you get all worked up, look again, okay?"

"Well, I'm supposed to be off at five, but it depends when Nancy gets here."

"Her kid's got a game after school."

"I don't have anything in the fridge at home—why don't you come down at five and we can eat something here."

"Pot roast."

"Minestrone."

"Lemon merengue pie."

"Okay. I'll see you then."

"Huh?"

"Oh, for God's sake, just look again!"

One Nation Under a Hat

THE SEVENTY-YEAR-OLD MEN ON THE park bench are as unlikely a pair as you'll ever see. Philmont Jackson is a a stylishly dressed black man who, despite having no particular place to go today, is wearing a three-piece, charcoal-grey pinstriped suit, brown Italian loafers, a matching lemon-yellow shirt, necktie, pocket square and socks—all topped off with a dark grey Borsalino fedora.

By contrast, Chaim Greenberg, a conservative rabbi, looks for all intents and purposes as if he slept in his rumpled black suit and used his hat for a pillow. The two men first met on this very spot some ten years ago, and, despite having virtually nothing in common, they have been enjoying each other's company for an hour or two nearly every afternoon since that day.

Today, they've exhausted the usual subjects— women; the weather; what's the matter with kids these days; how can a person leave the house wearing something like *that;* etc.

After a minute of silence, Greenberg has a question. "If you don't mind my asking, Mr. Jackson, how is it that you always manage to look so good in a hat?"

"Say what?" asked Jackson, surprised by the departure from the usual topics of conversation.

"No matter what kind of hat you wear on any given day, you look like a million dollars."

"Why, thank you, my man," said Jackson. "You really wanna know why that is?"

"Why else would a person ask if he didn't want to know?" asked the rabbi.

"Okay, here it is," replied Jackson. "A black man wears a hat; a Jewish man wears a hat, right? You're wearin' a hat; I'm wearin' a hat."

"Yes, of course," agreed Greenberg.

"The difference is that a black man wears a hat because he *wants* to wear a hat. A Jewish man wears a hat because he *has* to wear a hat. You see what I'm sayin'?"

"No, not exactly."

"Look—I can wear a hat or not. You *have* to wear a hat. God says you *got to wear a hat!*"

"Please go on," replied the rabbi, anxious to see where his friend was going with this line of reasoning.

"A black man, he wears a hat, and he be stylin'! See, I can wear any damn thing on my head—a nice fedora like this here, a beret, a do-rag, a flower pot, a bedpan—whatever I put on my head, I make it work. But *you*—you put on a hat, well, it ain't just the hat…"

"No?" asked the rabbi, now entirely intrigued.

"Hell no! Every time you put on a hat, it's like you got the whole weight of *God* on your head! How's a man gonna be stylin' with the weight of God on his head?"

<u>The Unexpected Guest</u>
(Trilogy, Part 2)

E VEN FROM THE FAR END OF THE WIDE, dry valley, the unmistakable rumble of the Peterbilt never failed to throw the dogs into an uproar. The trucker was glad to be home as he pulled the bobtail rig into the front yard of the creekside cabin he had built for his new bride some thirty years ago. The five overly acrobatic canines in the dusty yard could hardly contain themselves. Jumping down from the cab, the trucker tossed each one of them a strip of beef jerky— that always managed to quiet them down for a couple of minutes.

This time he had been away for three weeks. Throwing open the front door, he bellowed, as he always did, *"Hello, Mama—I'm home!"*

"Daddy!" she called out from the kitchen. She ran to meet him, reached up as high as she could and threw her arms around his neck. After three decades they still carried on like newlyweds. "Where've you been? I was expecting you hours ago!"

"Some poor driver broke down in Nevada and couldn't make it to Boise in time to pick up a reefer that had to get to Helena today, so a last-minute haul fell right in my lap. I felt bad for the guy, but I couldn't pass up easy money like that!" he replied. "I'm glad to finally be home, though, that's for sure!"

A big man, the trucker all but filled the doorway of the cabin. While suspended off the floor, out of the corner of her eye his wife caught an unlikely glimpse of what appeared to be an eagle feather suspended in midair behind his shoulder. When he finally let her down, she peered curiously around his elbow. Right behind him at her eye level was indeed an eagle feather. It protruded from the band of a straw cowboy hat perched atop the head of a brown and wrinkled little old man, his face framed by long silver braids.

"H-hello," she stammered tentatively.

"Hello, Missus," replied the little man, softly.

Her eyes turned to her husband. "Uh, Daddy— are you going to introduce us?"

"Oh, Mama, this is John Badger. He's a medicine chief! Isn't that something?"

"How do you do, Mr... uh, Chief," she sputtered.

"Pleased to meet you," he said, extending his right hand. "You've got a beautiful home here."

"Thank you. Uh… where are you from, Mr… Badger?" she asked uncomfortably, glancing back and forth to her husband, hoping for some sort of explanation.

"Way south of here—you prob'ly never heard of it," he said.

"I see," she said, still smiling awkwardly at the unexpected guest. "Mr. Badger, could you excuse us for just a minute?"

"Hey, Chief," interjected the trucker, "there's a real comfortable hammock out in the back yard by the creek. I'll bet you'd like to lie down and stretch your bones for a few minutes before dinner."

"Sounds good to me," said the old man.

"And don't mind the dogs," added the trucker. "They're all bark. Here's some jerky to keep 'em quiet."

After their guest had gone out the kitchen door and disappeared in a whirlwind of dogs and dust, the lady of the house spoke up. "Daddy, who is that man?"

"I told you, he's John Badger. He's an Indian!"

"Well, I can see that!" she said. "What's he

doing *here?"*

Well, you see," started the trucker, "I was kinda responsible for his daughter dumping him at a diner a few days ago, and before I knew it, he was riding with me."

"What on earth could you possibly have done to be 'kinda responsible' for someone abandoning her own father?" she insisted, incredulously.

"Well," he started, "they were sitting in the booth behind me, and she was giving him hell about spilling some juice or something. I couldn't see 'em, and I could only hear her, so I thought she was laying into a little kid, and you know how I hate that. So, I kinda poked my nose into it, and before I knew it, she got even more riled up and stuck me with their check and took right off and left him!"

"Couldn't you have called him a cab, or dropped him off at home?" she asked.

"No, he's had it with his daughter. She's mean as hell. They live on a reservation, and he's the last old-timer left. His wife, his friends, they're all dead. He just couldn't stand to go back out there."

"Well, okay, but I still don't see how this is your problem," she added, her tone somewhat softer. "Isn't there some kind of—I don't know—an agency or something?"

"Mama, he's a Vietnam veteran, just like me. And a Korean War veteran—*and* a World War II veteran, too! He served in three wars! *Three of 'em!* Don't you think we owe him something?"

"Well, sure," she replied, "but I was kinda hopin' to have you all to myself for the week."

"Look, he's been ridin' with me for several days, and he's no trouble at all. In fact, he's kinda, well, special. Can we at least feed him dinner and put him up overnight, and try to figure something out tomorrow? I mean, it's not like I do this kind of thing all the time."

She sighed deeply. "Do I have to remind you where each and every one of those five dogs out there came from?"

"Well, yeah," he said, sheepishly, "but this is different."

She sighed again. "Okay. He can stay tonight. Tomorrow, we figure out what to do with him. Your problem is that you're too soft-hearted."

"Yeah, I know," he blushed. "Thanks, Hon." He put his arm around her shoulder and kissed the top of her head.

When the trucker went to call John Badger in for dinner, he found him sound asleep in the hammock, the dogs stretched out calmly on the ground below him. That's a sight he had never seen before—all five dogs at rest. "Hey, John—you hungry?" he said, shaking the old man's shoulder.

"Huh? I sure am," he said, waking quickly. "What's for dinner?"

"Elk stew," replied the trucker. "Is that something you like?"

"Oh boy!" he said. "I used to eat a lot of that. Since I've been living with that daughter, seems like all we ever eat is sloppy joes and frozen pizza. Have I mentioned what a bad cook she is?"

"Yep, I think you might have," said the trucker.

The dogs followed the chief all the way to the house, transfixed.

"I've never seen these guys this quiet," commented the trucker, shaking his head.

"They're good dogs," replied the old man. "Real friendly."

The trucker had never thought of the dogs as either good or friendly. They put up with each other most of the time, and they had finally stopped barking at him and his wife every time they saw them, but he had never before seen them take to a stranger. For that reason, he always felt like his wife would be safe at home while he was away.

"John loves elk stew, Mama!" said the trucker as they sat down at the kitchen table.

"It sure smells good, Missus," said the old man.

"I hope you like it. My husband got this one last winter up in the Bitterroots," she said. "We've always got plenty of meat and garden vegetables in the freezer."

"All my daughter ever has in the freezer is hamburger and frozen pizzas," said the old man, ravenously shoveling in the stew. "She wouldn't know a fresh vegetable if it bit her on her fat butt. Oh— sorry, Missus."

"It's quite alright," she giggled into her napkin.

After a few minutes of silence, the old man said, "Missus, I been eating elk stew all my life, and I gotta say, this is the best I've ever tasted. The way you cooked it honors the animal's spirit."

"Why, thank you, Mr. Badger," she said. "That's as fine a compliment as I've ever gotten."

"Is that allspice and bay leaves in there?" he asked.

"Why, yes it is," she said, somewhat surprised. "And onions. They all go together quite nicely, I think. You have a good sense of taste."

"Thank you. I sure do enjoy a good meal," he replied.

Looking through the screen door at the dogs, the trucker couldn't help but notice how quietly they were still sitting. "I can't get over how good the dogs are being," he said. "They're not even picking on poor Moose with his bum leg."

"Oh, I think his leg is better," said the guest.

"Better?" said the trucker, quite surprised. "Not likely. He had a badly broken leg when I found him, and it's never been right since. We've had him to every vet in the county, and they all said he'd be limping for the rest of his life. I've even been thinkin' of takin' him to a young fella up in Kalispell—they say he can fix just about anything. No," he shook his head, "there's no way that leg got better on its own."

"You're talking 'bout the big brown one, right?" said John Badger, continuing to eat his stew.

"Yeah," said the trucker. "The poor guy seems so miserable sometimes, I just can't stand to see it."

"He looks fine to me," said the chief. "Go take a look for yourself."

"I'm telling you, it's impossible," said the trucker, excusing himself and walking to the back door. He threw a piece of jerky out the door, over the heads of the pack of dogs.

They all took off like a shot, the big brown dog at the head of the pack. Getting to the treat first, he proceeded to lead a lively game of keep-away around the back yard—without favoring the injured leg in the least.

"Well, if that don't beat all!" announced the trucker. "Mama, come look at this, will you?"

She joined him in the doorway. "What in the world? She said. "That poor animal has been lame for four years. Now he's running around like a pup!"

"He was sure limping when we got out of the truck," added the trucker. "John, do you know anything about this?"

The old man, still sopping up the gravy on his plate with a heel of home-baked bread, shrugged his shoulders. "What would I know about fixin' dog legs? Anyhow, since we got here, all I done is took a nap."

<u>Slap It Off</u>

"BOY, YOU BEST SETTLE DOWN BEFORE I slap the black offa you!" said the young mother, her patience gone.

"Mama," laughed the rambunctious young boy, "you know it won't come off!"

"You wanna see me try?" she shot back.

"No ma'am," he replied quietly.

"Alright, then. Sit down and hush!"

"Hush, hush, hush, hush!" was his reply.

"Boy, you are on my last nerve!" hissed the mother. "And you, missy—you sit right-side up and quit showing your fancy pants to everyone in the restaurant! Ain't nobody needs to see that!"

"Yes they do, Mama! *Everybody* needs to see my booty!" replied the little girl, standing on the booth's banquette and shaking her behind.

A quick swat to the frilled undergarment settled that argument.

Hippies, Greeks & Pizza

IT WAS ONE A.M. IN DOWNTOWN BOSTON ON a November night in 1973. The Grateful Dead concert at the Boston Music Hall had just let out, and the kids were hungry. The Greeks at the pizzeria had been on their feet all day and they were tired; the sudden flood of stoned, patchouli-scented hippies had them in an even worse mood than usual.

The disheveled young clientele poured in, mostly in groups of two or three. Ordering food off a menu was not something they were doing particularly well that evening. Standing at the chest-high counter, one of the kids ordered a couple of slices of cheese pizza for himself and his friend. As they waited, they laughed a lot and discussed, in broad, drug-addled terms, how unbelievably amazing the show was, and they both agreed how cool it would be if Jerry himself were to come in for a slice.

When the pizza was delivered, the boy discovered that it was not what he had ordered. "Oh, man, this has pepperoni on it," he said to his friend, sliding the paper plate his way. "I didn't want pepperoni. You want it?"

"No, man, I don't want it," replied his stoned companion. "What exactly is pepperoni, anyhow? It's too weird!"

The second boy distractedly slid the pizza further down the counter, where it was eagerly devoured by yet another stoned concert-goer, not a member of their party. Finishing both slices, he burped and left.

The man behind the counter returned to collect what he was owed. "Two-fifty," he said.

"Huh?" said the kid.

"Two-fifty for two slice pizza," said the Greek.

"I didn't get my pizza," said the boy.

"You order two pieces pizza, you owe me two-fifty," replied the counterman.

"No, man—I didn't want pepperoni," said the boy.

"Why you don't say something when I bring it? You eat pizza, you owe money."

"But I didn't eat the pizza, man!"

"Pizza don't fly away like bird!" said the Greek, who was growing impatient. "If you don't eat it, who eat it?"

The kid looked at his friend. "Did you eat it?"

"No, man. That pepperoni freaks me out!" replied the friend.

"There you go, man—we didn't eat the pizza," said the boy.

The irascible Greek said, loudly, *"You no pay, I call police!"*

"Fine, man, call the police," said the boy—a surprisingly bold move for a young fellow in his present condition. "We didn't eat any pizza!"

The Greek, who was far too busy for this kind of nonsense, started waving a 12" chef knife at the boys. "You *sonnamapeachy* hippie bum! I make you two pieces!" he said, angrily. "I make you face black!"

"Call the police, man," said the boy, with the presence of mind to know that dealing with a couple of tired cops would be preferable at this moment to any further interaction with the angry Balkan swordsman. "Let them figure it out."

Minutes later, two Boston cops arrived in response to the restaurateur's call. It was late, and they were tired. The night shift is bad enough, but an additional two or three thousand drug-addled kids really puts the cherry on the sundae. At least this was a change of pace from the public urination, drug sales and indiscreet public behavior calls they'd been dealing with in the neighborhood for the past several hours.

"Alright, Nick," said the senior officer, "what seems to be the problem here?"

"These damn bums eat my pizza and no pay for it!" said the harried Greek behind the counter, pointing at the two hippies with his chef's knife.

"First of all, my friend, let's put that knife down for now, okay?" said the officer. "Have you boys been drinking tonight?"

The boys looked at each other and giggled. "No sir, officer—not a drop."

"Alright, tell me what happened."

"We didn't eat any pizza, man," said the boy who had ordered the pizza.

"You lying bum!" said the counterman. "He order pizza, I bring pizza, I come back for money, pizza gone, he don't pay!"

"Okay, son, what happened to the pizza?" asked the cop.

"I don't know, officer," replied the boy. "I ordered two pieces of *cheese* pizza. He brought me two pieces of *pepperoni* pizza, and then he ran off before I could say anything about it."

"I offered it to my associate here, who also didn't want the pepperoni," said the boy, "so he pushed it aside and we waited for this guy to come back."

"And you didn't eat the pizza either?" the cop asked the second boy.

"No way, man!" replied the boy. "That pepperoni stuff? No way!"

"So neither one of you ate the pizza—is that what you're asking me to believe?" inquired the incredulous cop.

In a rare moment of clarity, the second boy suggested, "That's right, man—if you don't believe us, smell our breath! We haven't eaten any pizza tonight."

Short of pumping their stomachs, the senior officer couldn't think of a better way to actually prove whether or not pizza had been eaten—after all, it worked in a pinch for suspicion of alcohol consumption. "Okay," he said to his partner, "take a whiff."

"Me?" asked the junior officer.

"Yeah," said the sergeant, "the sooner we get this over with, the sooner we can get back out on patrol. Go on, now."

The younger cop moved close to the first boy and drew a deep breath. He smelled plenty of odd odors, but not a hint of garlic. "No pizza here, Sarge," he said. Moving on to the second boy, he did the same. "They're telling the truth."

"What I'm supposed to do?" asked the annoyed Greek. "I don't run soup kitchen here! These bums take my pizza and don't pay! *What I'm supposed to do?*"

"How much did you say they owe you?" asked the sergeant.

"Two dollar fifty cent!" insisted the Greek.

"Okay, my friend," said the cop. "Here's five dollars—two-fifty for the two missing slices, and two-fifty for a couple more for the lads."

"You gonna buy these bums pizza?" asked the counterman.

"For real?" asked the stunned and elated boys.

"Yeah, I want everyone to be happy," said the

cop. "Nick, I want you to stop waving that knife around at people, and I want you boys to feel free to come back anytime. Is that okay with everyone?"

"Seriously, Sarge?" asked the shocked rookie.

"Yeah," he said. "I've got three knucklehead sons of my own, and they occasionally get themselves in jams like this. I just hope that someone helps them out sometime."

The boys thanked the sergeant and took their two free slices of cheese pizza to go.

The cops returned to their beat, knowing that there were plenty more kids and plenty more messes awaiting them on the streets of Boston that night.

The Greek still had an hour before the place closed for the night, and an hour of cleanup after that. His opinion of mankind remained unchanged.

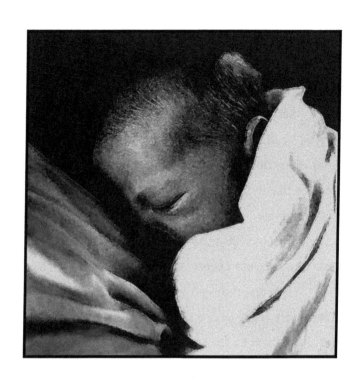

<u>Her First Grandchild</u>

"HELLO, DARLIN'! I'M SO SORRY I couldn't get here in time for the delivery. Are you okay? Did everything go alright?"

"Yeah, Mama, everything's just fine," she replied with a hug from her hospital bed. "The baby came a little earlier than expected, and I know you had a long way to come to get here. I'm so glad to see you! Did you have a good bus ride?"

"It was just fine; those new buses are real comfortable. Where's that baby?"

"You're just in time—the nurse just went to bring him in for a feeding."

"Oh, I'm so excited! My first grandbaby! And it's a boy?"

"A big, healthy, seven-pound, two-ounce boy!"

"Here he is," said the nurse, handing the baby to the beaming mother, who peeled back the blanket.

The new grandmother started to coo, then stopped and stared for a moment with her head cocked quizzically. "Darlin'," she said, "the nurse brought the wrong baby!"

"The wrong baby? Let me see," said the new

mother, holding him out at arm's length. "No, that's the right one."

"Darlin', this is a little *colored* baby!"

"Yeah, I know."

"But, Darlin'," she said, in a patronizing tone usually reserved for the very young or the intellectually challenged, "we're *white* people. You know how this works—white people have *white* babies. You don't just..." she stopped and gasped. *"Oh my God! Darlin'*, were you—you know...? Did you report it? Did they catch him? Is he in jail? It's not too late to put it up for adoption! *Oh, you poor thing!"*

"No, Mama, that's not what happened!"

"But then, you would have had to have... *Oh, Lord Almighty!* You would have had to willingly... have... with a..."

"That's right, Mama—*sex with a black man."*

"But, Darlin', how? *How in the world?* What about that nice boy Dennis you were engaged to— did you break up with him? Does he know about this? I knew something like this would happen if you moved so far away from home. Do you even know who the father *is?*"

"Yes, Mama, I know who the father is—and Dennis knows all about it."

"What kind of wild life have you been living here? I swear, it's like Sodom and Gomorrah!"

"Mama, relax! Dennis *is* the father."

"Dennis? But *how?* He's white!"

"Well, no, Mama, as a matter of fact, he isn't."

"But I've spoken to him on the phone dozens of times; I'd certainly know if he was colored!"

"Well, apparently not."

She paused. "And one of you couldn't have mentioned it just *once?*"

"Well, I knew you'd get upset."

"Upset? No, you're right—this is much better— wait 'til it's a done deal and *then* tell me! Oh, Lord! I've never even *thought* this before, but I'm so glad your dear father isn't alive to see this! What a nightmare!"

"Daddy would have loved little Lutie."

"Lutie? What kind of a name is that?"

"It's short for Luther."

"Luther? *Luther?!* You had the nerve to name this unfortunate little creature after your dear, late father?"

"Yep. Doesn't he kind of look like Daddy?"

"No, he most certainly does not! Do I need to remind you that your father was a *white man?*"

"Mama, you want me to ask the nurse if we can borrow you some linens?"

"Why on earth would I need linens?"

"To wear to your Klan meeting later."

"Oh, very funny!" she replied. "I'll have you know there isn't a prejudiced bone in my body!"

"Is that right?"

"Yes, that's right! All I'm saying is that there are plenty of—them—in the world, and they seem to be doing a pretty good job of keeping 'em coming. They certainly don't need your help!"

"Well, thanks, Mama—that's *much* better."

"Don't you understand? Your father was white; I'm white; all of your grandparents and great-grandparents have been white since the beginning of time."

"So?"

"*So*—you're our only child. Now, because of

this, all of our descendants will be black forever. *Forever!* They'll never be white again. It's like when you accidentally put one new red sock in the laundry with the white ones—none of them will ever be white again. *Ever!* Hundreds of generations of our ancestors are now spinning in their graves thanks to you!"

"Mama, what does it matter? Really—what does it matter?"

"Darlin', your ancestors came to this country so you wouldn't be European. They fought the Revolution so you wouldn't be English. They fought at the Alamo so you wouldn't be Mexican. They fought the War Between the States so you wouldn't be a Yankee. They fought two world wars so you wouldn't be German or Japanese. Your father fought in both Korea and Vietnam so you wouldn't be a communist Chinese, and now you've gone and, pardon my French, screwed up everything!"

"Wow! That's *some* history lesson, Mama. They never taught me half of that in school!"

"Well, you'll never be able to come back home, that's for sure. Most people there aren't nearly as open-minded as I am."

"Is that so?"

"Darlin', you know darn well it is. We've got our side of town, they've got their side of town, and that's the way it's always been."

"And you wonder why anyone would ever move away from there," mused the new mother.

"Where's Dennis from, anyway?" asked the grandmother. Where's his family?"

"They're on Oak Street, just off of Clinton."

"What a coincidence! We have an Oak Street that crosses Clinton back home, too—and it's also on *that* side of town. What are the chances of that?"

"It's the same one."

"The same one? Do you mean to tell me he's from back home?"

"Yep."

"How long have you known him?"

"Since kindergarten."

"How can that be? As I remember it, there was only one colored child in your grade. He was on the high school football team. Oh, your father loved to watch him play. He could run like the wind! The Midnight Train—that's what they called him—The Midnight Train. I forget—what was that boy's name?"

"Dennis."

She paused. *"That* Dennis?"

"Yep, *that* Dennis."

"Oh my God! Is that why you moved up here to the city? Did you run off together?"

"No, Mama, we actually ran into each other up here, just by accident. He came into the restaurant where I was waiting tables. You'll like him."

"I'll do no such thing!"

"You already know each other over the phone, and you've always told me what a nice young man he seemed to be."

"That was before he was black."

"For God's sake, Mama, he's always *been* black!"

"You know exactly what I mean! Does his mother know about all this?"

"No, not really."

"And why not?"

"Well, she doesn't exactly like white folks too much."

"I wonder why not?"

"I guess some of the women she's had to deal with at work have left a pretty bad taste in her mouth."

"Where does she work?"

"At Lurleen's Cut & Curl."

"Lurleen's? That's where I get *my* hair done!" said the new grandmother. "There's only that one colored girl there, and she *never* gets my hair right."

"That's her."

"I wonder what got her down on white folks?"

"Mama, one can only imagine."

The Chinaman Wins Again

"*S*ONNAMAPEACHY!*" SHOUTED THE YOUNG Greek as he threw the cards down on the table.

"What is it, Pete?" asked Liam O'Flaherty.

"Sonnamapeachy Tsinaman!" was the answer.

"Chinaman? Sure, my friend, there's no China-man here," replied the young Irishman, returning to the mournful tune he was playing on his fiddle. "It's just you and me."

"He tsit! Always he tsit!" said the Greek, to no one in particular.

"Pete, as surely as I'm sittin' here, there's no Chinaman anywhere to be seen," he assured him. "And it's just you, playin' the solitaire all by yourself, boyo!"

Pete muttered to himself in his native tongue and reshuffled the deck of cards. Though his given name was *Panagiótis*, he had given up on anyone on this multi-cultural crew ever being able pronounce it—thus, he chose the more familiar 'Pete'. His preferred evening pastime would be backgammon and a sip of ouzo, but there was no ouzo to be found out here in the middle of this western wilderness, and there was no teaching backgammon to these uncivilized shovel jockeys (or *chewtobákis,* as he called them) with whom he found himself. He didn't like the taste of their bourbon, but he would sip it with them just to be sociable. Truth be told, Liam didn't much care for the American whiskey either, but Irish or even Scotch spirits were also in short supply out here.

This was the nightly ritual in the mess tent of the rail camp; Pete would play solitaire by lantern light and curse his unseen opponent and O'Flaherty would play his fiddle and sip his bourbon. Pete had worked his way across the country from his landing point at Ellis Island—lining track for the Northern Pacific Railroad through Wisconsin, Minnesota, South Dakota and now Montana. His coworkers were mostly immigrants from places as far-flung as not only Ireland, but Wales, Italy, Sweden, and even Russia. Pete had come from Greece three years earlier to make his fortune.

Although now barely twenty, in that short time he had not only gained the trust of his employers, but had also proven himself to be better with numbers than the other boys. That had recently gotten him promoted from gandy dancer to paymaster.

When Pete first encountered the game of solitaire, he thought it was the most ridiculous thing he had ever seen. The ship's cook on his transatlantic voyage was an old Albanian named Dardan. He would sit on deck in his off-hours, rolling cigarettes and playing hand after hand. Occasionally, the games would end with a triumphant burst of laughter. More often, however, Dardan would throw the cards down and angrily bark, *"Mallkuar Kinez!"* before dealing another hand.

There were none of Pete's countrymen on board, so once he discovered that the Albanian spoke a bit of Greek, he began striking up after-dinner conversations with him. Finally, his curiosity about the one-man card game got the better of him; he had to ask about it.

"Is not one man play," said the Albanian in broken Greek. "Is two man play."

"But you're the only one I ever see playing," observed young *Panagiótis*.

"No, is me and *Kinezi*—Chinaman. He cheat—*always!*"

"Then why do you play with him?" asked the confused young Greek.

"Must win back money!" was Dardan's emphatic reply.

Pete had grown up a poor orphan in a small mountain village in Greece. He had set a virtually impossible goal for himself—he would marry Irene, the daughter of the richest and most influential man in town. One sunny day three years earlier he strode boldly up to the table in the open-air *kafeníon* where his prospective father-in-law was having his afternoon coffee. He introduced himself and proceeded to state his intentions—he would go to America, make his fortune, and return in five years expecting his betrothed to be waiting for him. The magnificently mustachioed older man was so flabbergasted by the nerve of this penniless upstart (not to mention the sheer impossibility of his plan) that he assented. There would be no great harm in feeding and housing a daughter for five more years until a more appropriate suitor came along.

Pete's new position as paymaster paid a bit more than that of a common laborer, and he was finally managing to save some money. Other than drinking, gambling and fancy women, there really weren't that many opportunities out here in the middle of nowhere to spend one's hard-earned money. When the other boys were off wasting theirs, Pete stayed in camp and played cards with the unseen Chinaman. As often as not, Liam would stay and keep him company. Sadness and longing being two things that know no national or cultural borders, Pete was even beginning to take a liking to the hauntingly sad Irish songs with which his red-bearded friend would serenade him nightly.

The young Greek's plan to return home and live like a king was derailed when his crew reached north-central Montana (which, even in the early years of the 20th century, was still largely uninhabited). An opportunity arose to which Pete had to give some serious thought; this endless landscape could be had for pennies an acre. Being an orphan, he had no family estate waiting for him back in Greece. In Montana, he could afford to buy land as far as the eye could see and still have enough money left to raise a family in relative comfort. This change of venue was bound to make his matrimonial plans a harder sell back in the village, but what young Pete lacked in pedigree he more than made up for in confidence.

As he watched the herds of antelope bounding over the foreboding yet strangely inviting expanse of purples and tans that stretched out under the garish orange and pink sunset, he thought that maybe he would start a ranch. And why not? He was in the Great American West now, and what would be more fitting than to become a cowboy? If that didn't work out, maybe he and his new bride would eventually settle in a bustling mining town and open a restaurant—maybe sell hamburgers like he had seen in New York City. Americans loved hamburgers.

And they would raise kids—lots of kids. Maybe one would become a teacher, maybe one a boxer—maybe one would be an official in the state government. Who knows—one might even become a doctor. The possibilities seemed endless here in the vast openness of this new land.

Now all Pete had to do was to make the long ocean journey back to Greece and convince his intended to leave her comfortable home and travel across the world to live with him among endless square miles of sagebrush.

At least this time he wouldn't be traveling alone. His unseen opponent would be with him, daring him to win back his hard-earned pay.

<u>Basic</u>

"AT EASE, JEMMINS," BARKED THE DRILL sergeant, scowling as he scanned the young faces assembled before him. "Y'all are, without a doubt, the sorriest excuses for military mens I have ever in my whole life had to babysit! I am disgusted just to see the uniform of the United States Army bein' so disgraced by hangin' offa y'all's flabby bodies!"

The new recruits stood impatiently, knowing that as soon as the sergeant was finished addressing them they would board a bus into town for their first pass since basic training had begun.

"Before I dismisses y'all, there is a couple of very important points y'all needs to hear," said the sergeant. "First of all, don't go bustin' nothin' up in town. I ain't comin' to bail none of y'all's asses out. You do some stupid shit like that, you gonna be coolin' your heels in the tank downtown. Y'all understan' me? You'll sit in a civilian jail until your hearin', then the MPs will come to get you and you'll have to go through a military hearin'. And then, who knows what might happen?

Y'all want that? *Do you?"*

"No, Sergeant!" came the response.

"Next, if you's plannin' to do any *socializin'*
while you's in town, make damn sure you put a jimmy
hat on your little troublemaker, you understan' me?"

"Yes, Sergeant!" snapped back the assembled men.

"Don't none of y'all needs to be makin' no child
support payments at this young age. And more important to me and the United States Army—a soldier
with a burnin' johnson is not a effective soldier. Are
we clear?"

"Yes, Sergeant!" they replied.

"I can't hear you!"

"Yes, Sergeant!" they replied in unison.

"One last thing before I lets y'all go," said the
sergeant, his eyes settling a little longer on the few he
was certain needed the advice. "If any of you badass
fightin' mens is plannin' to get yourself a tattoo, whatever you do, *don't get it where the judge can see it!*
Do all y'all understand me?"

The confused recruits looked back and forth at each other.

"Y'all don't understan' that?" asked the sergeant, shaking his head in disgust.

"Not really," they mumbled.

"Well," he explained, "Ain't nothin' says *'guilty as charged'* to a judge louder than a big ol' inky snake or spider or some such eyesore climbin' up outta your shirt collar. Now y'all understan' what I'm sayin'?"

"Yes, Sergeant!" barked the newly enlightened recruits.

"Alright then, ladies," said the sergeant, "try your best not to embarrass me and the United States Army. Dis—*missed!"*

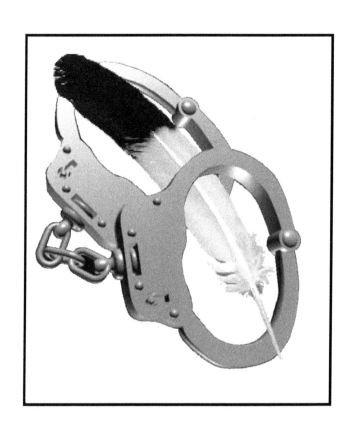

<u>Reunited</u>
(Trilogy, Part 3)

EARLY IN THEIR MARRIAGE, THE TRUCKER and his wife had agreed on a division of labor—he would drive the truck and she would stay home with the kids and handle all the business on the telephone. The truth was that he did not like to use the phone; being unable to see the face of the person with whom he was talking made him uneasy. Even his grown children knew that if they wanted to talk to their dad they had to drive out to the cabin and see him.

This morning, the telephone would not stop ringing. "Hon, are you gonna get that?" he called out to his wife. "Someone's calling, Mama—are you gonna pick it up?" The phone continued to ring.

"She went out," said Chief John Badger from across the kitchen table.

"Out?" said the trucker. "Where'd she go?"

"She took the dogs and went out to the creek to pick some of that watercress," said the old man, taking another sip of his coffee.

"Hell's bells," said the trucker. "I don't want to talk to anyone on the phone. John, you wanna get it?"

"No, not me," replied the old man, waving one

palm in front of him.

"Oh, all right," said the trucker. "That damn thing is about to drive me up the wall!"

He cleared his throat, picked up the phone and said, "Hello?" as politely as he could.

A female voice demanded, "Is this the trucker?"

"Pardon me?" he replied.

"I said, are you the trucker?"

"Well, I'm *a* trucker..." he said.

"What have you done with my father?" she yelled.

"I'm sorry, ma'am," he said with a smile, "I believe you have the wrong number. You have a nice day, now." He hung up the phone. "How about that?" he laughed. "Some crazy woman!"

The old man looked downward and shook his head. "It's Ray Anne."

"Huh?" said the trucker. "Ray Anne who?"

"My daughter. You remember—from the diner."

"How do you know it's her?" asked the trucker.

"I could hear her all the way over here," he said.

"Oh boy," said the trucker. "What do you suppose she wants?"

"My check," said John Badger.

"What check?"

"My government check. I get a nice fat check every month. My daughter ends up with the money — but without me there, she can't cash it." He chuckled, "She must be going out of her mind!"

The phone rang again. As much as he didn't want to, the trucker picked it up. "Hello?" he said, cautiously.

"You kidnapped my poor old confused father!" the woman on the phone yelled, even louder. *"What have you done with him?"*

"You know what, lady?" he said. "You haven't even told me who you are!"

"You know damn well who I am, cowboy," she said. "This is Ray Anne Badger from the Piñon Creek Reservation. What have you done with my father? I'm gonna have the State Troopers after you — maybe even the Feds — you took him across state lines! Are you asking for a ransom?"

"Now, hold on a minute," said the trucker, trying to gather his thoughts. With his hand over the receiver, he said to the old man, "John, you better talk to her."

"No, thanks," he replied. "You're doin' just fine."

"Damn it to hell, John!" replied the trucker. "She's really mad. She thinks I kidnapped you! She's going to call the Highway Patrol—and maybe even the Feds!" Taking his hand off the receiver, he said, "Now look here, Miss Badger, I did nothing of the sort."

"No? Then where is he?" she asked, her tone somewhat softer. "Is he alright? I've been so worried about him!"

"Well, he's here with me," said the trucker.

"I knew it! You did kidnap him!" she barked. "What have you done to him?"

"Now, look here, you!" he said. "Let's get this straight. You stormed out of that diner and stranded the poor old fella with no money and no way to get home."

"I came back after I cooled down and they said a trucker took him," she said. "It's took me a week to track you down, but here I am. What do you want from him? What kind of a pervert grabs a helpless old Injun and drives off with him?"

"Look," said the trucker. "He *wanted* to go with me. He *insisted!*"

"Let me talk to him!" she demanded.

The trucker handed the phone to the old man, who folded his arms and shook his head.

"Damn it, Chief," whispered the trucker loudly, "talk to her!"

"Nope," he said. "She can go to hell."

"Uh, miss—he doesn't want to talk to you right now," said the trucker.

"Alright, I'm calling the Montana Highway Patrol," she threatened.

"You just do that," said the trucker. "No one's done anything wrong. The truth is that poor old John got sick and tired of your crap and wouldn't let me drop him off at the reservation. He came with me of his own free will, and that's a fact!"

"We'll just see about that!" she snapped and slammed down the phone.

"Well, you old son of a gun," said the trucker, "what do we do now?"

The Chief thought for a moment. "She's like your dogs—all bark. She won't do nothin'."

"The last thing I need is trouble with the police,"

said the trucker. "My record is so clean you could eat off of it!"

"We'll be fine," said the Chief. "I'm sure of it."

After a few sips of his coffee, the trucker said, "Hey, let's get out of here before anyone else calls. Let's drive into Helena and I'll show you around."

"Sounds good to me," said the old man. "We can get out of your wife's hair for a few hours."

The trucker called out the back door, "Hey, Mama—John and I are going to drive into town for a bit. We're going to take the pickup. Do you need anything?"

"I know you'll stop at the Parrot for some lunch," came the reply. "Pick me out a box of mixed chocolates, will you? You know which ones I like."

"Sure thing, Hon. We'll be back by dinner time. Love you," he said. He didn't think he should burden her with the details of the earlier phone calls.

It was a beautiful day for a drive through the Montana countryside and into town. On the way they stopped in for a quick look around Frontier Town, a painstaking replica of an old fort perched on the east side of McDonald Pass. It was historically accurate enough that it made the Chief just a little bit uneasy. Once they reached Helena they made a few laps around the city, the trucker pointing out a few points of interest to his passenger—the Capitol Building, the Cathedral, the Historical Museum, the unique mosque-style Civic Center, the old fire tower, the train station, his childhood home, and the old steam locomotive he used to play on as a kid.

They eventually found a parking spot just off of Last Chance Gulch (which was never easy now that the main street had been turned into a pedestrian mall). The trucker didn't like any aspect of the urban renewal that had been visited on his hometown since the 1960s. The big quake in 1959 got people nervous about the possibility of old buildings falling down, and as a result a lot of his favorites, including the elegant Broadwater Hotel, the "Old Jeff" Elementary School that he had attended, the YMCA, and even the Marlow Theater, had been torn down—just in case.

The Parrot was the trucker's favorite childhood haunt; he had always felt at home here. The place was already old when he was a kid. The décor was somewhat Mexican; the dark wooden booths had the highest backs he'd ever seen. The ever-increasing collection of ceramic elephants still ran in a line of ascending size on the long shelf above and behind the counter.

"Come on, Chief. Let's get a booth; I'm starved," said the trucker.

"What do they got here?" asked the old man.

"They've got chili con carne, great big chicken tamales, and Mexican limes to drink," said the trucker, grinning excitedly like a young boy. "And afterwards, we can get some candy—they make it right here! And don't let me forget to get an assortment for my wife."

"That all sounds good to me," said the old man.

"Where've you been, stranger?" said the waitress. "And who's this?"

"Mary, this is my friend, John Badger. He's a medicine chief!"

"Well, how do you do, Chief," she said. "Pleased to meet you. What are you guys gonna have today?"

"Mary, we'll each have a bowl of chili, two tamales and a Mexican lime," said the trucker.

John Badger liked the place, especially the old railroad posters with Indian portraits on them. "Now, there's some good-lookin' guys," he commented.

"Mmm," said the Chief after a few bites. "This is pretty good stuff."

"I thought you might enjoy it," said the trucker. "I've been eating here ever since I grew teeth."

The two men had a leisurely meal, after which the trucker picked out a mixed box of chocolates for his wife, and he and the Chief got themselves a bagful to eat on the way back to the cabin. They did a little more sightseeing after lunch; they walked up and down Last Chance Gulch and saw some of the historic buildings, the trucker pointing out where some others had once been. They got the pickup and drove up as high as they could on the south end of town to see the panoramic view, including the Sleeping Giant, the recumbant rock figure forever guarding the north end of the valley. John Badger commented on how the sky really did look bigger here.

The trucker remembered a couple of items he needed from the lumberyard. On the way there, he showed the old man where he used to play little league ball. They took their time driving back to the cabin, just enjoying the beauty of the day.

From a mile down the road, the men could see that something was out of place at the house. There were cars—lots of cars—with lights flashing. As they reached the cabin, they could see that the entire drive-way and front yard were full of law enforcement vehicles of all sorts—county sheriff, state police, FBI, animal control, social services, and even the Bureau of Indian Affairs. As the two men exited the vehicle, they were greeted by a dozen uniformed men with guns drawn. The trucker recognized a couple of the sheriff's deputies as childhood friends of his sons. "Billy, Jimmy, what in the world's going on here?" he said. "Is my wife okay?"

Before either of the young deputies could answer, a Highway Patrol captain who the trucker didn't recognize stepped forward and said, "Sir, place your hands on top of your head and turn around, facing the vehicle."

"What's happened here?" asked the confused trucker, only then noticing that his wife was sitting on the front porch with her hands behind her. "Hon, are you okay?" he called out.

"Daddy, they've got me in handcuffs!" she called back, tearfully.

"Both of you need to turn around and place your hands on the hood of the vehicle," repeated the officer. Both men were patted down and cuffed.

"Will someone please tell me what's going on here?" said the trucker. "Why is my wife in handcuffs? And where are my dogs? Are my dogs alright?"

"They're all in the house, sir," said the trooper.

"Oh, no—they're not all supposed to be in there at the same time!" said the trucker. "They'll tear the place to shreds!"

"Sir, they had to be contained for everybody's safety," said the officer.

"Who's in charge here?" demanded the trucker. "Somebody'd better tell me what this is all about!"

The Highway Patrol captain said, "We got a complaint that an elderly Native American man named John Badger from the Piñon Creek Reservation had been abducted and was being held against his will at this address." Turning to the Chief, he said, "Sir, are you John Badger?"

The old man, who had so far been silent, spoke up. "You ain't gonna get nothin' from me but name, rank and serial number."

Stunned, the trucker said, "John, we're not in combat—tell these fellas what happened."

"Nope," he replied. "I know their game!"

"Come on, Chief, these guys are serious!" said the trucker. "You can clear this up right now! Please, John!"

The old man started reciting, "John Badger—Sergeant, United States Army—serial number..."

The state trooper interrupted, "Sir, a Miss Ray Anne Badger reported that her father had been kidnapped from a diner near her home. Are you that man, and are you, or are you not, being held here against your will?"

The old Indian continued to calmly recite his

military serial number.

"He's a little confused, officer," offered the trucker. "Damn it, John! Talk to him! My wife is sitting over there in handcuffs! *In handcuffs, John!* She's never even gotten a parking ticket in her whole life!"

"We have no choice but to take you all in until we get this figured out," said the state trooper.

"Please, officer, let me try to explain all this to you," said the trucker.

"I'm sorry, sir, you'll have to wait until the morning and explain it to the judge," said the Captain.

"This is all just a misunderstanding," said the trucker. "Last chance, John—talk to him before we all get hauled in! Do you really want to spend the night in jail?"

"I been a POW before," said the old man, defiantly. "The Geneva Convention says we don't gotta tell 'em nothin'!"

Before the trucker could respond, the officer said to each of them, "Get in the back seat. Watch your head." He proceeded to read them their rights.

"Do you really have to lock up the Chief? My

wife, too?" asked the trucker.

"Everyone goes until we get this straightened out," said the captain.

"What about the dogs?" said the trucker. "You can't leave them all in the house. There'll be nothing left to come home to!"

"County Animal Control will take them in to the kennel," said the officer. "They'll be alright."

The three were placed in separate cars—the trucker and his wife each in Highway Patrol vehicles, and the Chief with social services. Pending clarification, they were all taken to the County Jail, processed and locked up.

John Badger slept like a baby. In another cell, the trucker spent a fitful night wondering if his wife, locked up in a separate wing of the jail, was alright. When he finally did sleep, he dreamt of his five rambunctious dogs demolishing the interior of the cabin.

In the morning they were all taken in chains next door to the County Court House. More embarrassed than he'd ever been in his life, the trucker scanned the courtroom, hoping he wouldn't see anyone who knew him. Much to his surprise, seated in the back row was Ray Anne, the Chief's daughter.

"Court will come to order," announced the bailiff. "Please be seated."

"People versus William Jorgenson," said the judge. "How do you plead?"

"About what, Your Honor?" said the trucker.

"You are charged with the abduction of Chief John Badger," said the judge. "How do you plead?"

"This is all a big mistake, Your Honor," said the trucker. "No one got abducted!"

"How do you plead?" repeated the judge.

"Not guilty, Your Honor," he replied.

"Wendy Jorgenson," continued the judge, "you are charged with abetting, after the fact, the commission of a felony kidnapping. How do you plead?"

"All I did was to cook some meals and make up a bed for our guest," said the trucker's wife.

"Mrs. Jorgenson," said the judge, beginning to lose his patience, "how do you plead?"

"Well, I sure didn't kidnap anyone! And I didn't abet anyone either, whatever that is!" she said.

"How do you plead?" said the judge.

Before she could answer, John Badger called out, "Ray Anne, what are you doing here?"

"Order in the court!" insisted the judge, rapping his gavel on the bench. "Sir, you keep quiet—we'll get to you in a minute."

"Oh, okay," he replied. "How'd you get all the way up here to Montana, Ray Anne?"

"I flew," she said.

"In a airplane?" he asked.

"Order!" barked the judge, again pounding his gavel on the bench. *"Order in the court!* Now, I'm not going to tell you people again. I'm trying to conduct a hearing! If you want, we can take you all back to your cells and try this again tomorrow."

"I'm sorry, Mr. Judge," said the Chief. "That's my daughter back there. I'm pretty surprised to see her."

"I understand, Mr. Badger," said the judge, "but these proceedings must be conducted with a certain amount of decorum, do you understand?"

"No, not really," replied the old man.

"We have to do this by the book," explained the judge.

"Sure, okay," said the old man. "Mr. Judge, can I maybe come up there and talk to you for a minute?"

"Well, it's a little irregular," said the judge, "but if you think it will help me make sense of all this…"

"Yeah, I think it might," said the Chief."

"Well, alright. Bailiff, will you please help the gentleman up here?" said the judge. The old man shuffled up to the bench in his shackles. When he got there, the judge said, "Okay, Mr. Badger, what do you have to tell me?"

The Chief quietly began his explanation, "First of all, Mr. Judge, let's get something straight. No one got kidnapped—'specially me."

"Please go on," said the judge.

"Well, I don't really know where to start," said the old man. "I been livin' on the reservation with my daughter Ray Anne—that's her in the back row there— the fat Injun gal. She's not very nice to me. She's not very nice to no one. Anyway, we was eatin' breakfast at the diner down the road from the reservation. She got pissed off at me. Then the trucker—that's him over there – the big white guy—he tried to help, and she got pissed off at him, too. She left me there and drove off. That trucker, he's a really nice fella. He offered to drive me back to the rez, but I talked him into taking me with him instead."

"So, it was your idea to leave there with him?" asked the judge.

"Yup," he said.

"Please continue," said the judge.

"Well, we drove all over the West," said the Chief, his eyes widening with excitement, "back and forth through the mountains, droppin' things off and pickin' things up. I got to see a lotta places I never seen before. We come up here to Montana the other day—this is a beautiful state you got here. I been stayin' out at the trucker's cabin with him and his wife. She's real nice—cooks the best elk stew I ever had! You like elk stew?"

"As a matter of fact, Mr. Badger, yes I do," said the judge. "Please go on."

"She puts allspice and bay leaves in it," added the old man. "They mix with the onions and make the gravy really special. I never had it like that before."

"Sounds delicious," said the judge. "I'll have to get the recipe for my wife."

"You seem like a nice fella," said the Chief. "You and your wife oughta come out there and have dinner with us sometime!"

"Well, we'll see about that," said the judge. "Now please, Mr. Badger, let's get back to what happened."

"Well, I just wanted you to know that they're treating me real well," said the Indian, "not like that bad daughter of mine. Even the trucker's dogs like me—and they don't like no one at all."

"Yesterday, the phone started ringin' early in the mornin'," said the old man. "The Missus usually answers the phone, but she was out in the creek pickin' watercress. You like watercress?"

"Yes, I do," said the judge.

"I never had it before," said John Badger. "I don't think it grows around where I live. It's pretty dry there. That stuff is delicious!"

"Were you going to tell me about the phone?" asked the judge.

"The phone?" he said. "Oh, yeah. The trucker picked up the phone, and out of the blue, there was Ray Anne on the line! She started yellin' at him about me bein' kidnapped."

"What do you suppose caused her to accuse him of that?" asked the judge.

"Well, I think as soon as she realized that she couldn't cash my government check without me bein' there, all of a sudden she missed me," said the old man.

"Did you talk to her on the phone and try to straighten things out?" asked the judge.

"No, I didn't wanna talk to her," he said.

"Do you see how you could have probably avoided all this if you had talked to her?" asked the judge.

"Well, maybe I coulda," he answered.

"Mr. Badger, how does your daughter support herself?" asked the judge.

"Well, her husband—he's gonna be in prison for a while—he gets a disability check, and then there's my check," the Chief replied.

"So, she has no means of support of her own?" asked the judge.

"Her? She's too damn lazy to work!" said the old man. "She just sits around on her fat butt and spends money—his money and my money!"

"And why is her husband locked up?" asked the judge.

"What do they call it? Oh, yeah—domestic violence," he said.

"Is your son-in-law a dangerous man?" asked the judge.

"Him? No way. He's about the nicest guy I ever met, but he's not too bright," said John Badger. "She started it, then made it look like it was all his fault. She's not only a bad daughter, she's a bad wife too."

"Is there anything else you'd like to tell me, Mr. Badger?" asked the judge.

"Well, after Ray Anne called yesterday morning, the trucker took me for a ride around Helena. As big towns go, this one here's pretty nice. He showed me just about everything. We even had lunch over at the Parrot. You ever been there?" he asked.

"I've lived in Helena all my life, Mr. Badger," said the judge. "I grew up eating at the Parrot. My kids grew up eating at the Parrot. I take my grandchildren over there every Saturday. Now, if you don't mind, let's get back to the story."

"They even make their own candy over there!" said the Chief.

"Yes, I know," said the judge, with a smile. "My wife likes their dark chocolate cashew bark."

"Yeah, that's some good stuff," commented the old man.

"Please, Mr. Badger, go on," said the judge.

"When we got back to the cabin, there was all these cops waiting for us—with their guns out!" said the old man. "Pretty exciting! Then they hauled us all in."

"I see here that you were given an opportunity to straighten some of this out with the officers, but declined," said the judge.

"Well, I don't know if I 'clined exactly, but I didn't feel like talkin' at the time," said the Chief.

"Well, you sure could have saved yourself, the Jorgensons, and the Court a lot of trouble if you'd have been more cooperative with the police," said the judge.

"Yeah, maybe," said John Badger. "Sometimes you feel like talkin', and sometimes you just don't, you know?"

"I suppose so," said the judge. "Mr. Badger, where would you like to go when you get out of here?"

"Well, I sure don't wanna go back to that damn reservation with her if I don't have to," he said. "I'd kinda like to go back out to the trucker's cabin and take a nap in the hammock. This whole thing has kinda wore me out."

"I think I've heard enough," said the judge. "Bailiff, please help Mr. Badger back to his seat."

Once the Chief had gotten settled, the judge rapped his gavel a couple of times. "In light of new information I have just acquired from the alleged victim in this case, I am dismissing all charges against William and Wendy Jorgenson. Deputy, please remove everyone's cuffs and leg irons. There's some paperwork to be signed, but you are all free to go, with the apologies of the court. Case dismissed. Deputy, please see to it that they get a ride home right away. Bailiff, please bring

Miss Badger up here—we need to talk. Ma'am, do you have any idea just how much trouble you are in?"

In the hallway, together for the first time since their arrest, the trucker and his wife engaged in a tearful embrace. John Badger stood by for a moment, then began to laugh out loud.

"What the hell's so funny, you crazy old coot?" asked the trucker.

"I can't remember the last time I had so much fun!" said the Chief.

"Fun? We spent the damn night in jail!" said the trucker.

"Sure beats sittin' around on the porch waitin' to die!" said the old man. "And Ray Anne, I think she's in a heap of trouble. Yeah, this was fun."

"What did you and the judge talk about up there, anyway?" asked the trucker.

"I dunno," said John Badger, shrugging his shoulders. "We just talked."

"Well, he must've liked what he heard," said the trucker.

"I guess so," he said.

"We've got a lot to do today," said the trucker. "After we get home, we have to drive over to the animal lockup and get the dogs. I'm sure not looking forward to seeing what they did to the inside of the house yesterday."

"Oh my God, I forgot all about that!" said his wife. "It's going to be like a bomb went off in there!"

"Hey," said the old man, "I'm hungry. What's for lunch?"

<u>El Embrujo de los Viejos</u>
(The Spell of the Old Men)

IT HAD BEEN GOING ON SINCE BEFORE ANY-one could remember, and it might have continued forever had the president's wife not shown up that afternoon. Every Tuesday—and only every Tuesday—it was exactly the same. Through all the coups and the subsequent regimes it continued. Throughout the downtown business district, as if a church bell or a factory whistle or an imam had called them away from their duties, all the women would suddenly disappear. In every office and shop, in the library, even in the hospital, they would begin to twitch and fidget and glance at the clock—all of them at the same time.

One by one, secretaries, cashiers, seamstresses, nurses and librarians would announce that they had to run out for a moment to walk their neighbor's dog, or to take their mother to a doctor's appointment, or perhaps to just step out for some fresh air. Whatever their excuse, they would simply vanish.

On any given afternoon, the worn yet elegantly tiled bar on a cobbled backstreet off the square in the heart of the business district would be empty except for the bartender and the same two men playing back-gammon and drinking *café con leche*. But shortly after siesta time on Tuesday they would begin to arrive, always in the same order. Don Carlo would enter first with his coat over his shoulders and a little square suitcase in his hand. He would pause for a moment at the door and survey the scene before him, as if seeing it for the first time. He would then shrug and shuffle slowly to the same sunlit table at the front corner of the bar. Unsummoned, the bartender would bring Don Carlo a *caffè corretto*. The golden light of the afternoon stretched across his rumpled tan suit, transforming the tired old man into a glowing vision.

As Don Carlo sipped his fortified coffee, Don Paulo would arrive, carrying a longer, thinner suitcase. He would nod to the bartender and to the backgammon players, and then he would join Don Carlo at the table by the windows.

Without a word being spoken, the bartender would bring Don Paulo a glass—not a wine glass, but a beer mug—of red wine.

Next to arrive was always Juanito, carrying a big

lumpy duffle tied with rope, the shape of which hinted that it might contain a stuffed ostrich. Juanito was the only one of the group who ever smiled. Younger than the others, he was a huge man, given the diminutive version of his father's name when he was too small for anyone to foresee what an irony the name would one day become. He would extend two fingers sideways and wink at the bartender, who knew to pour him two fingers of brandy and no more. No sooner would Juanito get seated than El Gitano would arrive, carrying another thin rectangular case. The bartender would have an espresso waiting for him.

Always last to arrive was Don Gerónimo. Of all the cases the men brought into the bar with them, his was the only one whose shape immediately betrayed its contents; it obviously held a guitar. Of all the men, Don Gerónimo was the only one whom the bartender ever had to ask what he would be drinking.

He never knew right away—maybe a beer—no, perhaps a glass of Scotch whisky—no, maybe a mug of *mate*. After much tortured indecision, he would always settle on a bitter glass of *Cynar*. The five men sat together in silence, sipping their drinks and smoking French cigarettes and twisted little Parodi cigars.

After about ten minutes, Don Carlo would sigh and reach behind his chair and open his little square suitcase, from which he produced the beautifully aged, pearl-inlayed *bandoneón* that had belonged to his father, considered by many to have been the greatest player in the history of South America. Don Carlo would always warm up with a little Italian lullaby his father used to play for him when he was a baby; it was the first tune he had ever learned to play. The lullaby would continue as the other men opened their own cases, each containing another musical instrument: a violin, a mandolin, a double bass and, of course, Don Gerónimo's guitar.

One by one the women would gingerly enter the bar. In the blink of an eye, a room that had been all but empty filled to capacity. Lost in the music, the elderly musicians hardly noticed their delicately perfumed admirers.

After the lullaby, the group would play a few folk songs—some Spanish, some Italian—gradually escalating to some tarantellas and a few gypsy tunes. The women would close their eyes and slowly begin to sigh and sway as if in a trance. The afternoon light pouring in through the large windows bathed the crowd in a golden glow, giving them the appearance of a field of sunflowers waving in a gentle summer breeze. When, finally, the first strains of a tango began, an audible gasp arose from the audience, followed by a breathless silence. The women would forget to inhale and a giddy faintness would ensue; it was this moment that brought them here week after week.

It had caused somewhat of a scandal when *El Presidente,* then still a general, had married the beautiful and ambitious young showgirl thirty years his junior. But she seemed to make him happy, and when he was happy, the entire country breathed a little easier. On the afternoon of the day that would become known as *El Último Martes,* "The Last Tuesday", the First Lady was being driven through the business district on one of her weekly clothes shopping expeditions.

These trips were generally taken on Wednesdays,

but pressing business caused her to reschedule this week's outing to Tuesday. As she and her bodyguards stopped at the shop of one *couturier* after another, she became increasingly disappointed by the absence of her favorite shop girls. In a number of cases, they found the stores open but entirely abandoned.

After more than an hour of this eerily inexplicable wild goose chase, they happened to drive down an unfamiliar side street, a detour that took them right by the bar. Through the big front windows the First Lady recognized the seamstress from *La Mode Parisiènne*. Next to her was the clerk from *La Vestida Amarilla*. And next to her was her own social secretary, who had left work a couple of hours earlier, claiming to not feel well.

"¡Sinvergüenzas!" shouted the First Lady to no one in particular. "Shameless girls!" Angry and indignant, she ordered the driver to stop the limousine, and she ordered the two hulking bodyguards to wait on the sidewalk as she proceeded to squeeze her way alone through the crowd of women. She made her way to

where her social secretary stood. Normally, a public sighting of the striking young First Lady would cause a major disruption. Today, however, she went entirely unnoticed. She stood facing her secretary, who looked through her as if she were invisible. She looked around at the other women, whose demeanor was much the same. All they knew at that moment was that *los viejos* were playing the tango.

She spoke to the women, but there was no response from any of them. As she stood there, the music slowly began to overtake her as well. Her attitude began to soften, and she found herself turning to face the musicians, dropping her fur coat, loosening her collar and dancing dreamily in place like the others.

After ten minutes, the fearless bodyguards, both of whom had been with the president since his days as a young colonel, began to get concerned; if anything happened to *La Señora*, they knew the consequences for them would be, to say the least, dire. They pushed their way into the crowded room, only to find their charge swaying in the center of the crowd, a distant look of satisfaction on her face. Of all the eventualities for which these hardened soldiers had been trained, this was certainly not among them.

They flanked the First Lady and, each taking an elbow, gently but firmly escorted her through the crowd and back to the waiting limousine. *"Señora,"* they said, "are you alright?" She didn't answer. She merely stared ahead and smiled mysteriously.

The bodyguards drove the First Lady to *El Palacio*. When they gave the president their report about the afternoon's developments, he said nothing at first—he just squinted sourly and stared out the window of his office. To the guards' relief, he finally broke the silence. "Tango, you say?"

"Sí, Presidente."

"What is this place?"

"Just a bar, *Señor Presidente,* nothing special."

"And who are these men?" asked the president.

"Old men, *Generalísimo…* very old men."

"And the other men in this bar—the patrons?" he asked, suspiciously.

"We saw no other men, *Señor,* only women."

"What kind of women are free to go dancing

in the middle of a Tuesday afternoon? *Putas?*"

"No, *Presidente*, all the women in the business district—secretaries, teachers, shop girls, nurses—there was even a *nun!*"

"This is what goes on in my capital city? The citizens shamelessly abandon their duties and run wild in the streets?"

"Not all the citizens, *Señor*, just the women," replied one of the guards.

"*¡Bueno*—this will stop now!" said the president. "See to it."

"*Sí, Señor Presidente*, at once!"

The bodyguards returned to the bar with a personnel carrier full of the president's uniformed elite guard, whom they ordered to watch the door and let no one in or out. To their surprise, inside they found only the bartender washing glasses, and a faint memory of perfume hanging in the air—it was as if nothing at all had transpired there that day. The women were gone; the old men were gone; even the backgammon players were gone. "*Señor*," insisted the captain of the guard, *"las mujeres—los músicos—*where is everyone?"

"No sé, señor," replied the bartender.

"You don't know?"

"No, señor—no sé. They come; they go."

"Do you know who we are?" asked the big man in the ill-fitting blue suit.

"I'm afraid I do, *señor,*" replied the nervous bartender. Visits from *La Guardia Civil* were a dreaded part of the country's mythology—everyone had heard about them, but most were lucky enough to have never experienced them firsthand.

"Then you are aware that these visits don't always end well?" asked the captain.

"Señor, por favor," pled the bartender. "I have little or no control over who comes in here. *Los viejos* come in once a week, always on Tuesday afternoon. *No sé por qué*—they just show up."

"But, surely someone hires them," said the captain of the guard.

"No, señor—they just come. Ever since I can remember, they've come. It's like the seasons—or the tides. When I was a boy and my grandfather ran this

bar, they came—every Tuesday. And then the women show up out of nowhere—every Tuesday. *Los viejos tocan la música, las mujeres bailan.* Afterwards, everyone leaves and I straighten up the tables and chairs."

"*El Presidente* is not happy," said the captain. "He feels that this weekly fiesta is harming productivity and progress, and is thereby undermining the very fabric of our society. It could lead to revolution—maybe even communism. He orders it to stop immediately. From now on, there is to be no music played in this establishment. *¿Entiendes?*"

"*¡Sí, Señor Capitán—lo comprendo muy bien!*" replied the bartender, relieved that there had been no arrests or injuries.

"Alright, then—that's it for the music?" confirmed the captain of the guard.

"*¡Sí, Capitán, se acabó la música!*" The bartender assured him.

"*Ciao, señor.*"

"*Ciao, Capitán. ¡Muchísimas gracias!*"

As the two large men left the bar, the bartender crossed himself and said three Hail Marys.

The door opened once again; it was the captain. "Just in case I wasn't clear before, if it were to happen again, there would surely be arrests and the revocation of licenses — *¿Claro?*"

"*¡Sí, señor—muy claro!*" replied the bartender, nodding and grinning nervously.

Los Federales piled back into the personnel carrier and left as quickly as they had arrived. The bartender, who rarely sat down while on the job, collapsed into a chair and fanned himself with a dishtowel.

Later that night, facing each other from either end of the huge walnut table in the formal dining room of *El Palacio, El Presidente* and his wife sat, quietly sipping their *consommé*. "How was your shopping today, *mi amor?*" he asked.

The young woman continued to eat her soup, as if she didn't hear his question.

The president cleared his throat. "Did you not hear me, *señora*—how was your shopping?"

"Forgive me, *mi amor,* I was daydreaming," she said. "You will be glad to hear that my excursion was not very productive; I didn't spend one *centavo* of your money."

"What else did you do today, my love?" he asked.

"It was the strangest thing," she replied. "My secretary left early, complaining that she didn't feel well. Then, as I was driving down a side street in the business district, there she was, right in the front window of a bar, in a crowd of other women—dancing!"

"Dancing, you say?" he asked, feigning surprise.

"*¡Sí, bailando!*" she said. "On a Tuesday afternoon!"

"You'll have to have a stern talk with her tomorrow, no?" he said.

"*Bueno*—I had the guards stop the car, and I went inside and talked to her. It was as if she didn't even see me in front of her!" she said, excitedly.

"What could cause such behavior?" he asked.

"I'm sure I don't know," she replied, without a hint of ingenuousness.

Although the president found this very strange, he decided it would be best to drop the topic for now.

The following day, it was pretty much business as usual at the presidential palace. The First Lady turned her attention to the planning of her husband's upcoming birthday celebration. She fully intended to give her social secretary a firm talking to, but when their eyes met in the morning, all was forgotten and forgiven; the First Lady had, through no effort of her own, become a member of a strange unspoken sisterhood.

El Presidente liked it when the citizenry fussed over him on his birthday; it gave him the false impression that he was truly beloved. Compared to the flagrant corruption of the past regime, the population preferred the way the country ran now, but the fact was that they lived in fear of their new president and his inflexible form of law enforcement. His young wife, with unlimited resources at her disposal, couldn't have been happier than she was, being in charge of planning the following week's celebration. Hundreds of guests would be coming from not only all over the Western Hemisphere, but from as far away as Europe, Africa and even the Far East.

The *décor* would be provided by designers flown in from France, and the food, cooked by prizewinning chefs and bakers imported from around the world, would be nothing short of spectacular.

The only element now missing from the extravagant party plans was the music. Of course the National Concert Band would be present to play the national anthem and a few marches, but there would certainly have to be more. The First Lady left this matter in the hands of her staff, and in no time her social secretary came to her with an idea. As it happened, the president's birthday fell on a Tuesday this year. The secretary pointed out to the First Lady that since her husband's recent decree, *los viejos* were now probably available on Tuesdays; with a little bit of detective work she could probably track them down. The First Lady agreed that the music played by the old men was certainly as good a representation of the country's richly diverse cultural heritage as any she had ever heard, so she eagerly agreed that the search should begin. After the chilling visit by *La Guardia* to the bar, the neighborhood residents were not exactly eager to share information with strangers, but the First Lady's agents nonetheless began the persistent search for the elusive musicians.

The day of the party arrived and the grand ball-room of the palace had never looked grander. There were magnificently lighted fountains full of tropical fish; there were dramatic floral arrangements, some containing flowers never seen before in South America; there were cages full of exotic birds and animals; there were ice sculptures ringed by chilled shellfish. The international guests, many dressed in their native robes, were as varied and colorful a collection as the decorative flora and fauna.

The concert band struck up the national anthem. The room lights dimmed and a spotlight illuminated the top of the grand staircase. *El Presidente*, his beautiful young wife on his arm, entered and slowly made his way down the elegantly curved marble staircase. He was resplendent in his finest white dress uniform, replete with epaulets and a chest full of medals and ribbons. The First Lady was stunning in a strapless sequined floor-length blue gown that fit her toned dancer's body like a glove.

Once the couple had made their formal entrance, a receiving line was set up in order to give all the guests an opportunity to personally greet them. *El Generalísimo* knew that, at this moment, he was the center of the world's full attention.

In one out-of-the-way corner of the room, hardly noticeable amid all the splendor, was a quintet of musicians quietly playing the music of their nation. They started with a little Italian lullaby, followed by a few folk songs—some Spanish, some Italian. They gradually escalated to a few tarantellas and a few gypsy tunes.

The women in the room closed their eyes and slowly began to sigh and sway dreamily. When, finally, the first strains of a tango began, an audible gasp arose from the audience—followed by a breathless silence.

The Sink

ON A BUSY SATURDAY NIGHT, JOE EARL Parnell stood in the doorway of the men's room of the roadhouse he had owned and operated for seventeen very long years. He shook his head and sighed wearily, "Jimmy Ray, how many times do I have to tell you morons not to piss in my god damn sink?"

"Sorry, man," replied the offending customer, zipping up his jeans. "The toilets was all being used, and I had to go real bad. Plus, the sign was took down, so I thought maybe you done changed your mind."

"You thought maybe I changed my mind about people pissing in my sink?"

"Well, Joe Earl, the sign ain't there no more," said Jimmy Ray.

"And you're pretty sure it was me that took it down?" asked the weary proprietor.

"Well, it was you put it up, right?" asked the patron.

Jimmy Ray's logic made Joe Earl's head throb. "Okay—let's just say from now on, sign or no sign, that I would prefer it if no one pissed in the sink. *Do all y'all hear me?!*"

Various grunts of agreement came from all corners of the men's room.

"Alright then," said the bar owner. "Let's try to act like civilized human beings, okay?"

"Sorry, Joe Earl," was the general reply.

As he turned to leave, one last voice called out from one of the stalls, "Joe Earl, does that go for the ladies' room, too?"

The barkeep stopped in his tracks. Without turning around, he said, "Do you mean do I not want the *ladies* to piss in the ladies' room sink? Or do you mean do I not want *y'all* to piss in the ladies' room sink? 'Cuz I swear to God, if I ever catch one of you heathens pissin' in the ladies' room sink, I'm gonna skin 'im alive and *nail his balls up on the god damn wall!"*

After a brief pause, the voice behind the stall door replied, "Uh—never mind, Joe Earl. I was just sorta wonderin'."

The Author

ANTHONY S. MARKELLIS WAS BORN AND raised in Helena, Montana and now makes his home in Saratoga Springs, NY. A highly-regarded bassist and producer since the early 1970s, he has toured and/or recorded with such varied artists as Trey Anastasio, Paul Butterfield, The Mamas & Papas, David Bromberg, David Amram, Rosalie Sorrels, Paul Siebel, Kilimanjaro, The Unknown Blues Band with Big Joe Burrell, Esther Satterfield, Eric Von Schmidt, Johnny Shines, Michael Jerling, Bob Warren, No Outlet, Street Corner Holler, Mary McCaslin, Jim Ringer, Jo Henley, Rosanne Raneri, Floodwood and Krewe Orleans.

Markellis has always been fascinated by words—written, spoken and sung—English or otherwise. He counts among his friends writers and storytellers of all kinds—songwriters, authors, and playwrights—including a few Pulitzer, Grammy and Caldecott winners, all of whom have been a great inspiration to him. Mainly, he just pays attention to what goes on around him and tries to understand as much of it as he can.